FOLLOW ME DOWN
~ TO ~
NICODEMUS TOWN

Based on the History of the
African American Pioneer Settlement

illustrated by

A. LaFaye

Nicole Tadgell

Albert Whitman & Company
Chicago, Illinois

The *whoo-eeeh-follow-me* holler of the six o'clock train rumbled right into Dede's dreams. She rode across a prairie so wide even the angels couldn't see the end of it. Her family had a plan. They would own a place in that open land.

The Pattons wanted to leave sharecropping behind and have a farm of their own. They needed to make extra money to do it. When her day work was done, Dede's mama sewed dresses so fine, they practically got up and danced. Her papa worked the fields by day and built furniture by moonlight. And Dede made a shoe shine box to spiff up the shoes of the folks at the train station.

She watched shiny shoe after shiny shoe step into those trains, knowing the pennies in her pocket would pile up for years before her family could pay off their debt.

They all worked from sun-climb to sun-slide but still owed more than they made to the landowner, Mr. Sills. He kept them tied to his fields in a house they didn't own.

But good things come to those who pray.

That fall, Dede had spied a notice offering land for colored folks in Kansas. If they moved there and started a farm, they'd own it in a few years' time. The paper told of Nicodemus—a soon-to-be built town that'd be just a short wagon ride away.

Dede ran that notice right to her papa who said, "Why, Dede, you delivered a star we can hang our dreams on."

After that, they worked twice as long and three times as hard until their penny bank began to fill.

One afternoon, a man with his shoe half shined heard the last call to board the train. He ran off so quick he dropped his wallet. Dede scooped it up and raced after him, shouting the whole way. The man reached out the train window to claim it.

Turned out, Dede'd chased down a miracle. A letter came to the station for the "shoe shine girl" with a slip of heaven inside. The man who'd dropped the wallet had sent her a reward of ten dollars. Dede and her parents whooped and hollered enough to knock the nails out of the walls.

With Papa's furniture money, the cotton he brought in, and Mama's dress money, they had enough to pay their debt and stake a claim. Dede's shoe shine money would buy the seeds for planting.

They paid Mr. Sills and bid him good riddance, then stepped right up to the station window and bought tickets with the ten dollar reward money. Those little slips of paper felt like wings.

The Pattons boarded the train and rode off with their eyes set on the land they'd call their own.

In Kansas, they found a wheat-worthy prairie, and joining a group of fellow settlers, they took the final trek to Nicodemus together.

Working day by day, they dug themselves a home in the bank of the Solomon River. Dede was the first to use the door she helped her papa hang.

Papa and Dede marked the boundaries of their claim with stakes. Over the next few years they would have to prove up on the land— fence it, farm it, and register the deed. But now, with a full winter between them and the fields they needed to plow, the Pattons didn't have much more than the stars to guide them, stories to tell, and plans to make.

With a sling, Dede shot supper until even the prairie dogs grew scarce.

When their bellies set to biting, Dede went out with her papa to hunt further afield. She went over a rise and lost sight of the river, then came face-to-face with an Indian man taller than their house.

He held a rabbit in each hand saying, "Saw your chimney smoke go thin. Figured your food might be as scarce as your fuel."

That's how the Pattons met Shanka Sabe of the
Children of the Middle Waters. The white folks call
them the Osage, but they say they're the *Ni-U-Kan-Ska*.

The Pattons called themselves blessed for all that their new neighbors brought: food, fellowship, and the most precious gift of all—hope for the spring to come.

In the winter months, Mama set to sewing. Dede basted. Papa worked out where to plant.

When the ground thawed, Dede sowed seeds with Papa, planted a garden with Mama, and waited for things to grow.

When the pea-small prairie flowers started to bloom, plenty more folks poured into Nicodemus. The town went up like a revival tent—a new hotel, a bank, and a store. When Dede's family rode into town on Sundays, women slipped orders for churchgoing dresses into Mama's hand.

On occasion, Dede made a mail run into town. One afternoon, she heard Mr. Zachary say he had a full house in the hotel.

Taking a deep breath, Dede asked, "You think any of them folks need their shoes shined?"

Quicker than a wink, he plopped his own shoe on the chair. "I sure could use a shine."

And that's how Dede got a job shining shoes at the St. Francis Hotel.
Dede held posts for Papa, pinned prints for Mama, and tended the
garden, then shined shoes on the hotel stoop until the stars came out
to guide her home.

In a few years' time, the Pattons had fences up and fields harvested on the land they'd sown, thanks to the helping hands of the folks of Nicodemus and the Children of the Middle Waters. They could prove their land claim.

Papa let Dede carry her hotel shoe shine money all the way to the homestead office to register the deed. She brought the deed back to Mama and baby Gabe. They hung it in a frame Dede made from the prairie grass around their home. The place was now theirs, true and clear.

That Sunday, they had a party on the banks of the Solomon. Reverend Hickman prayed over their home. The folks of Nicodemus gathered at tables brought from every dugout. Shanka Sabe and his family arrived with all the food they could carry. Mama brought out enough pies to feed all of Kansas. And the Pattons finally had land to call their own.

But most important, they had a home where
they could tell stories, use the stars to guide them,
and make plans for the things to come.

ABOUT THE EXODUSTERS

When the Civil War ended, Jim Crow laws, unfair economic systems, and limited access to education made it extremely difficult for African Americans to live as equal US citizens. Sharecropping was one such unfair system, in which land owners assigned African American farmers and their families to small plots of land, charged them rent, and forced them to pay high prices for seeds, equipment, and basic necessities. This kept families in debt for years, unable to buy land of their own. At the same time, the Native American nations of the Great Plains were enduring the forced removal of their people from their land. In 1871, most of the Osage Nation were forced to sell the land they'd been given and relocate to Oklahoma. I based Shanka Sabe off one of the few members of the nation who were able to remain on the Osage Diminished Reservation.

Like the Children of the Middle Waters, African Americans wanted land of their own. The Homestead Act of 1862 gave them a unique opportunity because it offered settlers 160 acres of land, provided they could farm it, live on it for five years, and pay a small filing fee. Meeting these requirements was still challenging, especially for impoverished families, and many homesteaders relied heavily on the hard work and financial contributions of young children like Dede.

The African Americans who joined the land rush to frontier states like Oklahoma, Nebraska, and Kansas in the 1870s were called Exodusters. Their name came from the biblical story of Exodus when

the enslaved Hebrews were led to the Promised Land. In the US, these formerly enslaved settlers wanted to build their own promised land. Some Exodusters staked homestead claims; others went to work on farms. Nearly thirty thousand resettled in Kansas alone. They were partly motivated by the work of individuals such as Benjamin "Pap" Singleton, known as the Father of the Exodusters, who formed an association encouraging African Americans to leave Tennessee for the frontier.

These African American settlers faced natural, financial, and racial hardships to build a better future for themselves. To increase their chances, many banded together to build their own communities like Nicodemus, Kansas, which was founded in 1877 by the Reverend W. H. Smith, a white land developer named W. R. Hill, and five other African American men. It is the oldest and only surviving Exoduster town.

Today several descendants of the original settlers of Nicodemus still live in the area. The town is now an unincorporated community in Graham County, but some of the original buildings still stand. Nicodemus became a National Historic Site in 1995 due in large part to the efforts of historian Angela Bates and others. Each year the current residents, the families of former residents, and the descendants of the original settlers celebrate the Nicodemus Emancipation and Homecoming during the third week in July.

You can learn more about Nicodemus and the amazing people who settled there at https://www.nps.gov/nico/index.htm.

To all those who braved the odds to find their own place.
Like our girls, Adia and Katie.—AL

For the descendants of the original Nicodemus pioneers,
and to all dreamers who share the spirit of hope—NT

Library of Congress Cataloging-in-Publication data is on file with the publisher.

Text copyright © 2019 by A. LaFaye
Pictures copyright © 2019 by Nicole Tadgell
First published in the United States of America in 2019 by Albert Whitman & Company
ISBN 978-0-8075-2535-7

Printed in China
10 9 8 7 6 5 4 3 2 1 HH 22 21 20 19 18

Design by Ellen Kokontis

For more information about Albert Whitman & Company,
visit our website at www.albertwhitman.com.